l a u r e n   c h i l d

I am TOO absolutely small for school

CANDLEWICK PRESS

for Sofie and her
invisible friend
Søren Lorensen

and for Maisie, Clemmie,

Molly and Ella

Absolutely thank you to Goldy

For taking all the photographs so beautifully Thank you to Simon

Catalog for his utterly invaluable comments Library of Congress

Catalog Card Number 2003065576. ISBN 978-0-7636-2887-1 (paperback).

edition 2005. Library of Congress Cataloging-in-Publication Data is available.

The illustrations were done in mixed media.

99 Dover Street, Somerville,

First published in Great

Printed in Shenz

WKT 15 14 13 12 11

China. This book was typeset in Officina serif Book and Badloc.

14 15 16 17 18

London.

Massachusetts 0214

ick.com

www.candle

She says,

"I probably do not have time to go to school. I am too extremely busy doing important things at home."

I say,
"At school
you will learn
numbers and how to
count up to **one hundred**."

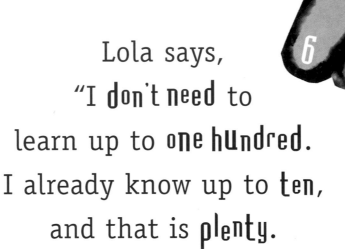

Lola says,
"I **don't need** to
learn up to **one hundred**.
I already know up to **ten**,
and that is **plenty**.

I have **ten** fingers. And
also I have

ten toes.

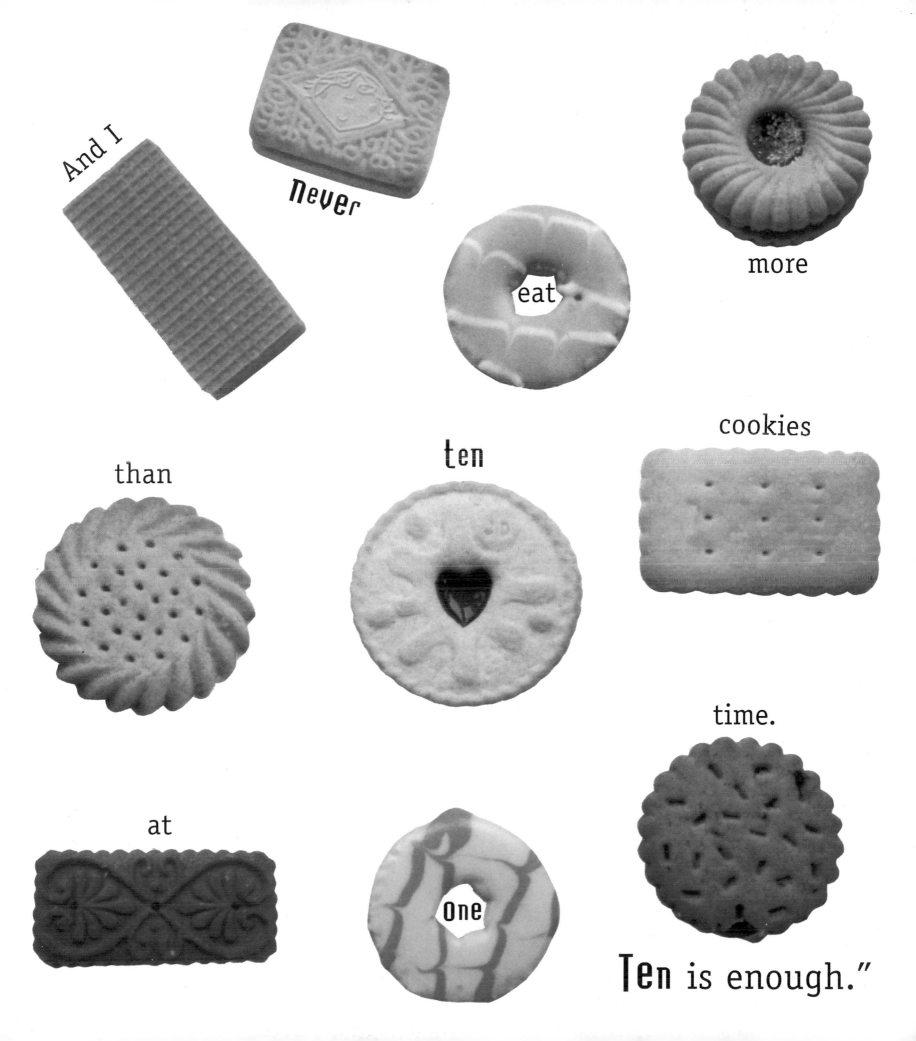

And I

Never

more

eat

cookies

than

ten

at

One

time.

Ten is enough."

"But Lola," I say, "what if eleven eager elephants all wanted a treat.

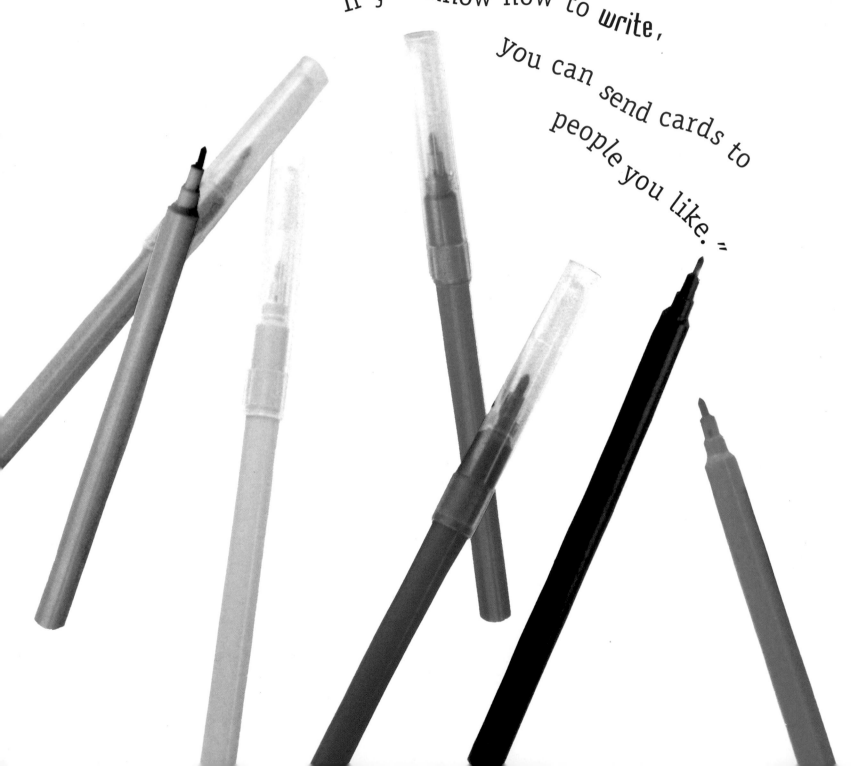

I say,

"And what about learning your **letters**, Lola?

If you know how to write, you can send cards to people you like."

"But not everyone has a telephone, you know, Lola," I say.

"Who doesn't?" says Lola.

"Santa Claus," I say. "You have to write him a special note and send it to the North Pole to tell the elves your Christmas wish. Otherwise the elves might get your wish mixed up."

"I didn't know that, Charlie," says Lola.

"And Lola," I say,
    "don't you want to
read words? Then you will
        be able to **read** your
own **books**. And understand
secret messages written
on the fridge."

Lola says,
    "I know lots of **secrets**.
I don't need to **read words**,
        and I've got all my
books in my head.
    If I can't remember, I
can just make them up."

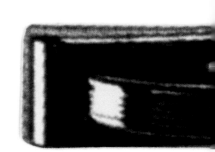

"But Lola," I say, "what would you do if there was an ever-so-angry ogre who would not go to sleep unless you read him his favorite bedtime story?"

"I don't know, Charlie,"

says Lola.

Then Lola says,
      "I would like to
read to an ogre and
      count up elephants and
send notes to the North Pole.
But I absolutely will NOT
      ever wear a schooliform.
I do not like wearing the
same as other people."

I say,
      "But Lola, you
won't have to wear a
      school uniform. At our
school you can wear
            whatever you like."

"Oh," says Lola.
      "You wait there. I know
exactly what I can wear. . . ."

"Well, Lola," I say, "that's certainly stylish,

but you **cannot** go to school dressed as a **crocodile**."

Lola says, "This is **not** a **crocodile**. This is **a alligator**."

I say, "You can't really go as **an alligator**, either."

"Why not?" says Lola.

"I like to wear stripes," says Lola, "but what will I do at lunchtime? You know I will **never** NOT EVER eat a **school lunch**."

My sister, Lola, is fussy about food.

I say,

"But Lola, you can take your very own **packed lunch** in your very own **lunch box**."

Lola says, "I do not want to eat at school, **alone**, all by myself, on my own."

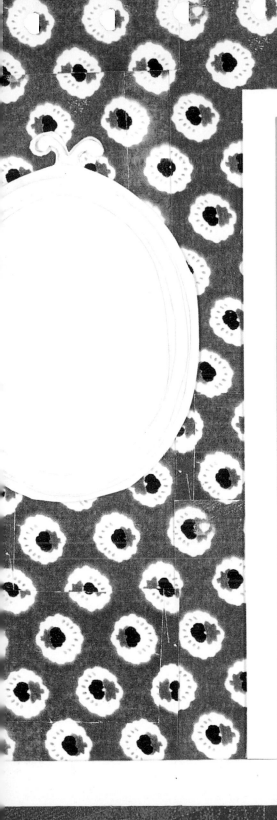

I say, "But Lola, at school you will meet lots of new **friends**. You can have **lunch** with one of them."

Then Lola says, "But I already have **my friend**, Soren Lorensen. I like to have **lunch** at **home** with him."

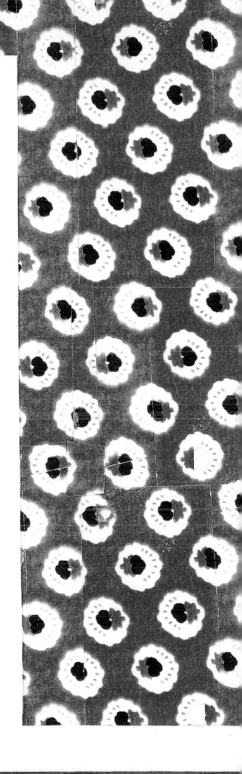

Soren Lorensen is Lola's invisible friend. No one knows what he looks like.

Walking to school, Lola is all wobbly. She says, "Soren Lorensen is feeling slightly not very well. He is worried he will not be able to count numbers, do letters, and read words, and no one will

"Lola," I say, "it will be okay. You'll be fine. I bet you'll both have a really good time. And after school we'll have pink milk at home."

talk to him, so he will be all by himself, on his own."

But all day I am **worried**.

I don't see Lola at recess,

and she's nowhere at lunch.

When school gets out, she's not by her peg.

But then

there

she

is,

and she's

not all alone,

by herself.

She's

hopping

along

home

with

somebody

else. . . .

At home, I say,
    "Lola, I **told you** that you would
        have a **good time**."
And Lola says,
    "Oh I know, Charlie, I was not
worried. It was Soren Lorensen
        who was nervous, **not me.**
    I was **fine**."